"PROCLAIM LIBERTY THROUGHOUT ALL THE
LAND UNTO ALL THE INHABITANTS THEREOF..."

– LEVITICUS 25:10

www.MysticWatersPublishing.com

... --- ... / - .... . / .- -. ... .- . -. - .. -. -. . /

--. .- -. .-. . -.-- / .. ... / ... .. -. .- .- .. -. --. / .. -. /

- .... . / -... .- - ... - --- / ... --- ...

Mystic Waters Publishing © 2009

Lucy's Great Adventure © 2011

All rights reserved.

ISBN 13: 978-0-9824498-2-0

ISBN 10: 0-9824498-2-8

LCCN: 2011925827

First Print June 2011

Regal Printing Limited

Published in Margate City, NJ

On file at the Library of Congress.

1 2 3 4 5 6 7 8 9 10

LUCY'S GREAT ADVENTURE

WRITTEN BY

STEVEN PAUL WINKELSTEIN

ILLUSTRATED BY

CHRISTIE MEALO

Mystic Waters Publishing • Regal Printing Limited

OTHER WINKLE BOOKS

Elephant, Elephant Come Alive!

The Diving Horse and the Magic Whistle

Available at www.ElephantAlive.com

POST YOUR PICTURES!

E-mail a photo of you holding 'Lucy's Great Adventure'
at a spot featured in the book:

Photos@ElephantAlive.com

See YOUR photo at www.ElephantAlive.com!

acKNOWLeDGeMeNTS

The Author
My family, The Markmans, Richard Helfant, Neil Cirucci,
Christopher Hartney, Elana Lalasis, Dee Sawyer, Bobby, Malelani Cafe,
The infinite wisdom of the Coffee Klatch, The Madonna, Skittykitts,
Katie Catanio, Jay Schultz, & The Bat.

The Illustrator
My family for supporting my passion, my friends for entertaining and inspiring me, and my many wonderful teachers and mentors for helping my creativity blossom.

MeMORY & DeDiCaTiON

In Memory Of
Richie Gargel
&
Amy Nicole Hauck

I dedicate this and all of my work to the Ocean, which

guides me, and to the Moon, which guides the Ocean.

'Twas a morning in Margate one early July,

when Lucy the Elephant looked to the sky.

And what did she see, but a horse that could **FLY!**

She had seen

it with both

of her big bluey eyes.

The horse played a flute, just a toot on the flute,
and Lucy felt Wiggles and Squiggly Woots!
There were Biggles and Giggles inside of her boots,
right down to her very last elephant roots.

"Come alive," said the horse. "Wake, wake, **WAKE**!
You must save the island, from the Slithery Snake.
Lucy, lift up your toes. Shake, shake, **SHAKE**!"

So, Lucy woke up and she rubbed her new eyes.

Then she stomped and she stamped and she shooed away flies!

But her keeper, R. Helfant, was shocked and surprised!

"Sinatra! Sinatra! My Lucy's alive!"

3

"There are tasks you must do,"
the high horse he did say,
"You must do, you must do,
you must do on your way!
They are tasks- **neigh, neigh,
NEIGH**, that will help save the
day..."

He whispered three tasks
into Lucy's right ear.
Not even the elephant
keeper could hear.
The horse was then off
with a neigh and a wink.
Flying high in the sky,
he was gone in a blink.

Before Lucy's journey, she wanted to eat. So, she marched on her feet to a place that had sweets. Something cold and delicious, an elephant treat!

"I am off! I am gone!
Two Cents Plain! Two Cents Plain!"
Where she ate so fast,
she froze her elephant brain!
"Oh, the pain! But the taste!
It's too good to complain!"

With a "Thanks!"
and a "Bye!"
Lucy truly began.
To the
Green Bridge
of Margate
was where
Lucy ran.

On the street called Jerome
she was warned by a mole,
"Beware! At the bridge you will find an old troll,
a nasty old troll, who will charge you a toll."

6

"Oh, my!" Lucy said, and she blasted her trunk,
which scared the poor troll to the bay, where he sunk!

"I'm sorry," she said.

"Here's some change for the fee."

But the rest of the day all the cars rode for free!

8

The signs guided Lucy to where she should go.

A place where our freedom was sown long ago.

"Philadelphia!" Yes!

Where that flying horse said,

"Feed your head, feed your head!"

What that flying horse said!

9

Then a sound! What a sound! Twas a tummy tum **CRUNCH**.

"Cheesesteaks!" said Lucy, "What a yummy yum lunch!"

"Wiz Wit for the cheese and the onions," said Pat.

And she scarfed them with ketchupy squirts- splat, splat, **SPLAT**!

After sipping the river, a share that was fair,

Lucy walked through the beautiful Rittenhouse Square,

where she passed a bronze statue,

a whispering goat;

"Baa quick, baa baa Lucy, the Sea Snake it comes,

the Sea Snake it comes on a slimy sea boat.

To Market Street now, where her first task awaited,
where Liberty's Bell swings cracked, copper plated.

RING, RING, RING, RING!

She rang it four times like the horse once had said,

which woke Lady Liberty and her green head.

As the light went away and outside became dark,
lovely Lucy the Elephant ran through Love Park.

In a fountain
she tossed away
all of her cares.
Then, Lucy ran up the Art Museum stairs.

Next stop was the train station, Thirtieth Street.

Where she squeezed

her round **bum**

in a tiny

t r a i n

seat.

They arrived in the night,

to a new shiny city,

where the place was all lights

that were bright and were pretty,

where people would climb to the top of the heap;

it was New York City, where the fun never sleeps!

On the street was a shirt Lucy bought with an I,

she bought the shirt then with the N and the Y,

with an I, and an N and a Y, and a heart.

Then she bought some fresh nuts from a man in a cart,

a man, Lucy learned, was a man they called Bart.

Then Lucy was off on her Twinkle Tink toes,

moving on, moving by, as she followed her nose.

Central park in the dark
and the place where we skate,
and she climbed
up the building
of our Empire State.

Lucy saw Lady Liberty, standing so high,

with a crown on her head and a torch in the sky,

and as Lucy looked further a book in her arm,

and her face was alive, by the Bell's rung alarm!

"Elephant, elephant, tell me why have you come?

Why am I alive? Tell me what have you done?

I'm the Statue of Liberty, elephant, see?

I'm the Liberty, Justice, and Truth by the Sea."

"Lady Justice of Truth!" shouted Lucy so loudly,

"I ask that you ride back home with me proudly,

on my back, to a place where our freedom's in trouble.

Let us

fly,

let us

fly,

let us

fly,

on the

double!"

Lucy's second task done,

and the Statue climbed on,

with a **smack**

from the great copper book

they were gone!

But the scene that they saw

when they came riding in,

was the scene

of the Slithery Snake

slitherin'.

23

None were allowed
out of their own houses;
not adults, not children, not dogs,

and **not** mouses.

"You, Slimy Sea Hisser,
be gone and make haste!

For I am the strongest of all you have faced!

I'm the Lady of Freedom so leave, Slimy Snake.

If you don't disappear, it will be a mistake!"

With a super big shout
from her elephant throat.
Lucy chased that old Sea Snake
right back to its boat,
and off of the island and out to the sea,
where that Slithery Serpent
was supposed to be.

When the third task was finished they all left their houses;

the adults, the children, the dogs, and the mouses!

They praised the great Statue for being so witty,

and Lucy was given a key to the city!

They danced all about

'till the time came for bed,

when Lucy,

she rested her elephant head.

She smiled as she drifted away,

back to sleep,

a long sleep that would keep,

such a sleep-

Deep, deep, deep.

www.eLePHaNTaLive.coM

www.faceBooK.com/TheWiNKLe

www.MYSTicwaTeRSPUbLiShiNg.com

www.TwiTTeR.com/TheSLiTheRYD

Don't forget!

E-mail a photo of you holding 'Lucy's Great Adventure' at a spot featured in the book:

Photos@ElephantAlive.com and check it out at www.ElephantAlive.com

A very special 'Thank you!' to Christopher Hartney, Lucy the Elephant's official, award-winning videographer for providing this photograph, for his video services to The Winkle, and for making Lucy's eyes glow.
Long live the Boys of the Howdah!

.--- .- .. / --. ..- .-. ..- / -.. . ...- .- / --- --